Albert's Very Unordinary Birthday

To Nanna F, Grandma L and Poh-Poh Y, thanks for all the food, love and stories.
And to Daniel B, who takes all of the above and turns it up to eleven.
In loving memory of Uncle A.

This edition published by Kids Can Press in 2018

First edition 2018, originally published in Australia and the UK under the title *Grandma Z*.

Text and illustrations © 2018 Daniel Gray-Barnett

Published with the permission of Scribble, an imprint of Scribe Publications
18–20 Edward Street, Brunswick, Victoria 3056, Australia

Kids Can Press gratefully acknowledges the financial support of the Government of Ontario,
through the Ontario Media Development Corporation for our publishing activity.

Published in Canada and the U.S. by Kids Can Press Ltd.
25 Dockside Drive, Toronto, ON M5A 0B5

Kids Can Press is a Corus Entertainment Inc. company

www.kidscanpress.com

The artwork in this book was rendered in pencil and ink and colored digitally.
The text is set in Handegypt and Archer.

North American edition edited by Yvette Ghione

Printed and bound in Shenzhen, China, in 3/2018 by C & C Offset

CM 18 0 9 8 7 6 5 4 3 2 1

Library and Archives Canada Cataloguing in Publication

Gray-Barnett, Daniel, author, illustrator
    Albert's very unordinary birthday / written and illustrated by
    Daniel Gray-Barnett.

ISBN 978-1-5253-0118-6 (hardcover)

I. Title.

PZ7.1.G73Al 2018   j823'.92   C2018-900765-6

Albert's Very Unordinary Birthday

Daniel Gray-Barnett

Kids Can Press

On an ordinary day,
in an even more ordinary town,
it was Albert's birthday.

Every year, no matter how much
he wished it were different ...

... it was just like every other
extremely ordinary day.

"A robot piñata? Bake a cake?
Oh dear, no!" said his mother.

"You know how your father feels
about mess.

Now, why don't you put on your
birthday socks?"

"Balloon poodles?
Musical chairs?
Oh dear, no!" said his father.

"You know how your
mother feels about noise.

Now, how about some
birthday toast?"

Albert closed his eyes and imagined himself
at a birthday party, holding a piece
of chocolate-cherry-ripple cake.

Then he made a wish.

Knock, knock, knock!
Albert's mother jumped.

Knock, knock, knock!
Albert's father jumped.

Knock, knock, KNOCK!
Albert opened the door.

Standing there was a strange woman.
But Albert knew who she was.
He had seen her in the old photo albums.

It was his grandmother.
It was Grandma Z.

"Happy birthday, Albert," she said.
"Chocolate-cherry-ripple is a
marvelous choice. Shall we go?"

Albert got a fluttery feeling in his stomach,
like one hundred monarch butterflies coming out
of their cocoons. His skin began to tingle.

"Oh dear, no," said Albert's parents.
"You know how we feel about the unordinary!"

But Albert didn't want to spend his birthday like every other day.
"Grandma Z," said Albert, "where are we going?"

"Well," said Grandma Z,

"You are most definitely going places!

But today, we're just off to do some ordinary birthday things."

Albert's parents breathed a sigh of relief.

Albert and Grandma Z went hunting for Dew of the Sea,
Thunder plants and Dead Man's Bells.

They climbed Enchanted Rock.

At the curiosity shop, Mr. McQuillen showed Albert the dragon's tooth horn.

They played in the Midnight Forest.

They went bird-watching,

and Albert spotted sandpipers on their way to Siberia.

They visited a palace with twenty-four bedrooms,
six fountains, a jungle-room,
a planetarium and a pastry chef.

The King and Queen of Osternovia found them so delightful,
they asked if they could stay for the summer.

They taught Icelandic horses how to can-can, rode the Big Dipper seven times in a row and discovered a new species of beetle.

"Albert," said Grandma Z,

"There's one more thing this day needs to be truly special."

After the party was over, Albert and Grandma Z went home.

"The next time my day starts to feel ordinary," said Grandma Z, "I know who to visit."

"My goodness!" cried his father.
"What on earth happened to you?" said his mother.

"I had a very unordinary day," said Albert.

"And it was wonderful."

From that day on,
whether it was his birthday
or any other day, for that matter,
Albert never felt ordinary again.

Not once.